Jody the mouse, is a magical toy. He was fashioned by The Wizard of Paint Creek. The Wizard is a skilled toy maker, who endows his toys with magical qualities - qualities only apparent to children with imagination.

Jody understands and speaks every language there is. He, and all the other mice that the Wizard made, know many wonderful things, which they share with those who believe in them.

Katie Murphy believed in Jody from the start. He became her family's guide on their trips through Michigan.

Jody's Michigan Adventure Books tell about all the things that happened to Jody, and Katie's other animal friends. You are invited to come along with the Murphy family. All you need to do is enter into Katie's imagination . . .

Great Places
Jody's Michigan Adventures
Michigan's Upper Peninsula

Summary: One hot summer day, Kevin and Katie
Murphy remember the magic of Tahquamenon Falls
in Winter. Their mother tells them they are going to
the Upper Peninsula for a suprise vacation. Katie
talks Jody, her toy mouse, into going along. In the
middle of Kitch-iti-kipi, Katie drops Jody in the
springs as a bear swims toward her and her brother.

Written by Leigh A. Arrathoon & John J. Davio
Illustrated by Kenneth M. Hajdyla
Coloring by Mary Anne Strong

If you want more information on
Great Places, write for a free brochure
Paint Creek Press, Ltd.
P.O. Box 80547, Rochester, MI 48308-0001

ISBN 1-893047-04-0

Printed in China

Katie Murphy

Kevin Murphy

Jody

Mike Murphy

Mary Murphy

Alfred

The sun was burning hot. It was July 2nd. My little sister, Katie, and I were on the back porch, drinking lemonade. My name is Kevin Murphy, by the way.

"This summer is so smothering and so long. I can't stand it," I complained.

"You're always going on about the heat. Why don't you put your feet in a bucket of water?" Katie was disgusted with me.

"I don't want to sit. I want to <u>do</u> something," I said. I was bored. "I want to go on an adventure."

"Hmmm." My sister sighed. Her eyes were far away and dreamy. Me, I was so bored I thought my head would explode.

"What are you thinking about?" I asked her.

"Do you remember when we went up to the U.P. last winter?"

Well, yeah, I guess I did remember. We drove up through Mackinaw City. It was snowing. It was about 10 degrees - not 90, like now.

We ate at a restaurant there. Of course Katie couldn't sit still. Even though she was seven, she still had to get up and wander around. Naturally she found out they have a store there with lots of stuffed animals.

"Oh Daddy!" she cried. "I have to have a moose. If we're going to the U.P., a moose is just what I need."

My father wanted to keep the peace, I guess. "Ok," he said, "but that's all you get to buy the whole time we're gone, so make sure it's something you really want."

"Oh yes. Oh yes!" Katie cried. And that's how we got Alfred. Alfred is this brown velvety moose, with a weird face. I couldn't see what she saw in him.

After we left Mackinaw City, we took the bridge across the straights. It was cold and windy.

"Yeah, I remember," I said out loud. "Man, it was cold."

"The best part of the trip," Katie said, "was Tahquamenon Falls. It looked like a fairy world. Everything was covered with fresh snow. The trees were parading in their white fur coats. Don't you remember?"

She stretched out her arms and tilted her head, pretending to be a fashion model. I guess she was supposed to be a tree. The pines had about six inches of fresh snow all over them. You could see the green peaking out from underneath. Every so often, a tree would get tired of the weight and shake some of the snow off.

We walked about a mile from the parking lot. It was so cold. My nose was numb. Katie was carrying Jody, the stuffed mouse my dad bought her in Holland, Michigan - he has a jacket. The moose, Alfred, got to stay in the car because he didn't have any warm clothes.

When we got to the first overlook, Katie was so impressed that she dropped poor old Jody on his head. The view was beautiful, but cold. She never even noticed Jody was missing.

The first glimpse we got of the Upper Tahquamenon Falls was through the trees. We were in this dark place looking out. The water on the top of the falls was the color of slate. When it rolled over the top, it was white, with dark orange streaks. My dad said the streaks came from the tannic acid in the water. This acid is **leached** (filtered or washed) from the tamarack and cedar trees that grow on the banks. Anyway it was an awesome sight.

"Do you remember the stairs down to the falls?" sighed my sister. "It was like a narrow passageway into a magic kingdom!"

"Ok." I said. I know better than to waste my breath arguing with Katie. "What I liked best was when we got down the steps. There was the waterfall. It was so big, and the water just gushed, even though parts of it were frozen."

"Yeah, there was ice right up to the bottom of the falls." Katie said. Then she added. "You know what? We should ask Mom and Dad if we could go back there. I mean there was so much we didn't see. We should go there on our vacation."

My mom was making dinner. Katie and I came rushing in to see what she thought of our idea about going to the U.P. for our vacation. She laughed when we told her what we were thinking.

"Why are you laughing? I was dead serious," Katie pouted.

"Me too," I said.

"I'm laughing because that's where we're going next week. I was keeping it as a surprise, but I guess it's all right for you to know."

Katie was so excited that she ran right upstairs to tell Jody and Alfred.

"Oh no!" said Jody. "I had enough of that place. You forgot me, and I had to stand on my head in the snow for a very long time."

"We came back for you," Katie soothed. I just got excited when I saw the falls."

"Well, there were other things I didn't like. For example, that great lump of a moose got to stay in the car. Now do you think that was fair?"

Alfred had nothing to say about this. He just stood placidly, chewing his cud.

Katie eventually persuaded Jody to go on the trip. Alfred was coming too, of course. He smiled because he was looking forward to seeing some of his relatives. But Mich, the toy turtle from Mackinaw, refused to have anything to do with our plans.

"I'm not going swimming in the straits again!" he snorted. The black bears swim across the water whenever they please. No thanks!"

It was the first time my sister had thought about bears.

"Mommy? Do they have bears in the U.P.?"

"Oh. Yes they do sweetheart. And you must promise not to pet them if you see them. You must also promise to stay very close to Daddy and me because bears are not always friendly creatures."

"But the little bears are cute, aren't they Mommy?"

"Yes, but the little bears are born in January, while the mother is hibernating. By July, most of those little bears aren't so little any more. They're still 'cubs,' - that's the name for 'little bears' - but they weigh at least 25 pounds by mid-summer."

Katie eventually persuaded Jody to go on the trip. Alfred was coming too, of course. He smiled because he was looking forward to seeing some of his relatives. But Mich, the toy turtle from Mackinaw, refused to have anything to do with our plans.

"I'm not going swimming in the straits again!" he snorted. The black bears swim across the water whenever they please. No thanks!"

It was the first time my sister had thought about bears.

"Mommy? Do they have bears in the U.P.?"

"Oh. Yes they do sweetheart. And you must promise not to pet them if you see them. You must also promise to stay very close to Daddy and me because bears are not always friendly creatures."

"But the little bears are cute, aren't they Mommy?"

"Yes, but the little bears are born in January, while the mother is hibernating. By July, most of those little bears aren't so little any more. They're still 'cubs,' - that's the name for 'little bears' - but they weigh at least 25 pounds by mid-summer."

"Well, that's not very big," protested Katie.

"No, but by the time the mother wakes up from her winter's sleep, she's very protective of her cubs. If you pet one of her little ones, she might get angry and come after you."

"Oh, oh." said my sister.

"The mother can weigh between 300 and 350 pounds. The father weighs about 500 pounds."

"That's pretty big, isn't it Mom," I said.

"Yes it is. And the male bear can be <u>very</u> unfriendly, so please don't either of you wander away from us even for a moment. Is that agreed?"

We both nodded.

* * *

We set out in the dark. When we got to Mackinaw City, it was 9 a.m.

"I need a bear," Katie said to our father, as we passed the gift shop on our way to breakfast.

"You already have a toy for each arm. That's enough!" my father said. And that was that.

The very first thing we did when we got across the Mackinaw Bridge was to stop in St. Ignace. My father said a lot of the local people there were descended from French trappers and **voyageurs** (French canoe paddlers).

I learned that in 1634, Jean Nicolet passed through the Straits looking for a route to the Orient. Soon afterwards, the Jesuit priest, Father Jacques Marquette, founded a Mission at St. Ignace. It was called St. Ignatius Loyola, after the founder of the Jesuit Order.

French traders had begun coming into the area. Father Marquette wanted to convert the Indians to Christianity. He was worried when he saw them trading their valuable, warm beaver for alcohol.

Indians were protected from liquor by law, but the laws were hard to enforce. Around 1812, settlers' cabins sprang up. Many of these people had their own private stills. Indians simply got their drinks from them rather than from traders.

We went to the Museum of Ojibwa Culture. We learned about the Ojibwa (Chippewa) way of life. These people thrived in the cold, northern climate. The lifestyle of the Huron and Odawa (Ottawa) was shown by a Huron longhouse. These Indians had **to migrate from** (leave their homes in) Southern Ontario when they were chased by the Iroquois.

The Ottawa and the Hurons settled around Georgian Bay, while the Chippewa and Ojibwa clustered on either side of Eastern Lake Superior.

Actually, the Chippewa settled at **Bawating** (place of the falls), later called Sault Sainte Marie. The Potawatomi (or keepers of the fire) lived in what we now call Southern Michigan.

Every summer, 3,000 members of the Great Lakes tribes gathered at Bawating to trade. They played ball games. The Indians used sports as a way of training warriors. They also gambled. Is this why the Chippewa are so prosperous with their casinos today?

The Indians pampered their children. Lessons were learned from grandparents' stories and example, rather than from physical punishment.

These people hated miserly ways. They valued generosity and sharing.

The Ojibwa believed in a Master of Life. All living things, rocks, trees, winds etc., had spirits to commune with the Master on behalf of the Indian. Aseenewub, an Ojibwa, wrote:

> These are the words that were given to my great-grandfather by the Master of Life: 'At some time there shall come among you a stranger, speaking a language you do not understand. He will try to buy the land from you, but do not sell it; keep it for an inheritance to your children.*

This old Indian prediction foretold the arrival of the European on American soil.

We went to the Indian Village too, where they sell rubber tomahawks.

"You're going to be even more boring when you grow up, aren't you?!" Katie yelled at me. "When are we going to get on with our trip?"

*Reader's Digest, **Through Indian Eyes: the Untold Story of Native American Peoples**, 1995.

Our father took U.S. 2, which goes west, on the south side of the peninsula. You pass by beautiful, sandy beaches. It was hard to know which place was best. We finally decided to camp in the Brevoort Lake Campgrounds, in the Hiawatha National Forest. My dad liked it there because they rented **kayaks** (Eskimo canoes). In fact the two of us went kayaking while my mother and sister sunbathed.

My sister had heard that **Kitch-iti-kipi** (the big spring) is really neat. Since it was on our way to Fayette - a ghost town my dad promised we could visit - we went to this place first.

Kitch-iti-kipi is a beautiful, emerald-green spring. It's about 200 feet wide. And it's as clear as crystal.

"Now we get to see something!" Katie humphed at me as we trudged through the forest.

"This place is like a storybook," she gasped. She looked around at the cedar and pine forest with wonder.

The spring looked like an oval-cut emerald. We got to the middle of the water by pulling ourselves along a cable that was attached to the raft we took.

"Look! Huge fish are swimming around. I can almost touch those mossy logs. See 'em?" my sister yelled.

Katie and I were both good swimmers. We were all alone in the middle of the spring. Our parents were waiting at the water's edge. I had the feeling that something was watching.

"Hey, Kev!" I heard my sister whisper harshly. "Look over there!"

I whirled around. For a moment I didn't see anything, and then I spotted it. A black bear had been drinking the spring waters. It was very big.

"Oh, oh," said Katie. "It's good we're out on the lake."

The bear put its long nose in the air as though it were trying to sniff out its dinner, which I think was us.

"Didn't somebody tell us they could swim?" I asked.

"I don't know," shrugged my sister.

"We'd better get back to shore quick," I said.

Just as I began pulling on the rope, the bear decided to go for a swim in the spring. I pulled as hard as I could, but it seemed as though the bear was getting closer and closer. Jody was dangling from Katie's hand, over the side of the boat. My sister was pretty scared. She let go of the mouse. He tumbled into the water.

"Ohhhhhh!" she cried.

"Never mind!" I yelled. "We can get another mouse."

"No we can't. Oh Jody!" she wailed. "Jody is magical!"

The mouse drifted away, smiling.

When we got to shore, Katie was crying very hard. My father picked us both up, and the four of us got back to the car so fast I couldn't even say how we got there. My sister couldn't stop sobbing.

"Here," said our mother. "Hold Alfred. He's all alone. He can't understand why no one pays any attention to him."

"I don't care about Alfred. I want Jody!" Katie cried.

"He's gone," our father said, and his voice sounded hollow as though we had just lost our best friend.

Alfred smiled stupidly at us. He just didn't care about anyone but himself. Katie was disgusted with him. Jody had been part of our family for three years. He'd been our guide everywhere we went. He spoke "Hollmouse." What could Alfred do beside smile?

"He speaks Finnish," our mother said brightly. "That's why he hasn't spoken to you. He doesn't understand English."

"Finnish?" we were both surprised.

"Yes. See the best thing about the Upper Peninsula is that there are so many interesting people here," said our mother. "Let me read to you."

Our mother read to us about the people who came to Northern Michigan to mine and cut lumber.

The Cornishmen came to work the copper mines when their English copper and tin mines no longer produced. They brought their famous meat pasties (pastry with meat, turnips, potatoes, and onions). They heated these on their shovels, which they held over their candles when they were down in the dark mines.

The Finlanders introduced the steam bath, or sauna, to the U.P. They came to mine too, but later took up farming. During logging days, they worked in the lumber camps. They brought their language with them. It so influenced local speech, that many people up here have a strong Finnish accent. They talk like this even when they're not from Finland.

The people with Finnish accents are known as "Yoopers." "Yooper" clothes are tough woolens that last a lifetime, You can buy these at Albert's in Ironwood.

"Jody would have liked that," said my sister. She was depressed.

"Of course there are many different kinds of people living here. There are quite a few Swedes. They came to Ishpeming and the mines around Iron River and Ironwood. They also settled in Baraga County. The village of Skanee is Swedish," our mother said. "There were Hungarian, Polish, Italian, and Belgium immigrants too."

"Italians?" my father interrupted. "What does it say about them, Mary?" His mother was Italian, so he was interested in this.

"Yes, Mike. It says they worked in the iron mines of Dickinson, Marquette, Iron, and Gogebic Counties. Father Mazzuchelli of Milano was an early Italian missionary. Many Italians went into business. They stayed away from the lumbering camps, which were mostly Scandinavian."

We had arrived at Fayette. This was the ghost town I had been waiting to see. Even though there are a lot of abandoned towns here, Fayette is the only one that has ever been restored. I could hardly wait to see the old homes of the 19th century Jackson Iron Company workers.

Fayette boomed between 1867 and 1891. There was a store, an office building, a superintendent's house, barns, a machine shop, nine frame homes, a hotel, an opera house, and forty log houses. I guess 500 people lived here when charcoal pig iron was being produced.

At first they had a dense forest. They used up all the wood to fire their furnaces. Then they had several accidental fires that badly damaged the furnaces. It was finally because iron production was so low that the town began to close down. But it survived until 1950 as a resort and then a fishing village. By that time, the forest had grown back and the people had all moved on. We had to peer through the windows. The houses were still being restored, so we couldn't go inside.

We stayed at the campground that night. Katie just couldn't forget Jody. She slept fitfully. In her sleep, she had a dream about him. She told it to me.

"In my dream, I went back to Kitch-iti-kipi to find Jody." she began. "I couldn't leave him there."

"I pulled the boat out to the center of the spring, but the mouse was nowhere to be found. So I went back to shore. I decided to walk around the spring. When I got to the other side, I saw the huge black bear that had chased us, taking a nap. Then I saw two cubs, wrestling in a meadow.

'Hey! You guys!' I yelled to the cubs. But they didn't hear me.

I walked up to them and pulled one of them by the ears.

'Ouch,' it said, quite annoyed.

'Where's Jody?' I asked him.

The bear was puzzled, but his sister knew what I meant.

'Oh, the little mouse,' she said (in Yooper), 'he's right there.' She pointed with her paw.

Sure enough, there was Jody, sitting with a third little bear, laughing. I grabbed him and started back toward the spring. Unfortunately, the big bear was very angry. She was standing right in front of me. I was afraid she was going to eat me. She was growling, showing her huge fangs. That's when I woke up."

"You just had a bad dream," said our mother soothingly.

"No, it was a message. I'm supposed to go back to Kitch-iti-kipi," said Katie. "Wouldn't you go back and look for me if I were missing?"

"Of course I would," our mother cried. "I'd never stop looking until I found you, but . . ."

"Then I have to go back and look for Jody," Katie interrupted, and that was that.

* * *

Our father made us stay in the car while he went to look for Jody. He was gone about a half hour. We were all getting pretty worried. Then, at last, he appeared. He was carrying something in his hand all right. It was a very water-logged stuffed mouse.

From that moment on, Katie was like a little mother, nursing the mouse back to health, feeding him bits of our supper, keeping him covered with a blanket. It was sickening. I was so glad the U.P. is rich in things to see. Otherwise I might have spent my entire vacation watching Katie slobber over Jody.

There was so much to see! We toured the Tilden Mine to learn how they used to extract iron ore. We also got to see **taconite pellets** (made from iron ore) being loaded into the boats from the train at Marquette.

We visited the Hanka Homestead, a Finnish farm in the Keweenaw Peninsula. Katie and Jody became "Yoopers," heaven help us. They talked in Finnish English and wanted to buy Yooper clothes. After that we went to the Quincy Mine Hoist to learn how they mined copper.

My dad took us to the Soo Locks to watch the big ships being transported from Lake Superior to Lake Huron, or vice versa. Lake Superior is 21 feet higher than Lake Huron, which is why the ships have to use the locks. They can't navigate the falls.

We also saw the Point Iroquois Light Station at White Fish Bay. The Great Lakes Shipwreck Historical Museum is right there too. Some day I'd like to see the wrecks under water. But of all the wonderful things we saw, the best were Pictured Rocks and the Gogebic waterfalls.

"Gogebic," by the way, is Chippewa Indian for "where trout rising to the surface, make rings on still waters." Pretty, isn't it?

The Porcupine Mountain Wilderness State Park has old-growth, **primeval** (of the earliest times) forests. This is because it was too expensive to **log** (cut timber) there. It is the most beautiful place I have ever seen, for sure.

After our meeting with the bear, my father didn't want to take any more chances. Instead of hiking to the falls, we followed short, easy paths from the parking areas.

There are four waterfalls on the Presque Isle River in Gogebic County. These are Manido, Manabezho, Nawadaha, and Iagoo. My favorite was Manabezho.

The water roared over a 20-foot ledge. I guess the river is 150 feet wide there. The largest section of the falls is golden, and there was a lot of foam. There was fern and moss on the steep cliff wall surrounding the falls. I really loved it there.

Above Manabezho Falls is Manido Falls. The drop is about 25 feet, after which the water turns into rapids. You can look downstream and see Manabezho Falls. Upstream is Nawadaha Falls. Nawadaha Falls is like a jewel, made out of lacey white foam.

It was peaceful in Gogebic County - until my sister saw a "Wookie."

"Wookie?" I said.

"Yes! He looks just like the guy in Star Wars," she answered.

My father quickly picked her up and whisked her off to a safe distance. The "Wookie" was a porcupine, and it was not pleased at having my sister for company.

"Porcupines throw their quills when they get mad!" my dad said.

"I throw things too, if I'm mad enough," replied my sister, with a shrug.

"No, no! You don't understand. Those quills are sharp. If they stick in you, they really hurt."

"Oh," answered Katie thoughtfully. Then, when she'd mulled it over, she added, "That's not very nice."

"The porcupine doesn't care if he's being nice or not. He throws his quills to protect himself. He's scared when he does that."

Katie was concerned. She wanted to speak to the Porcupine, to tell it she meant it no harm. My dad sighed.

"Let's go!" he said.

On the other side of the U.P., between Grand Marais and Munising, was one of my favorite places on this trip - Pictured Rocks. It was so awesome, I don't know how to describe it.

We took a Pictured Rocks Cruise so we could see the rock formations. Reddish iron, blue-green copper, and other deposits form a colorful layer which stands out against the sunset.

Miner's Castle is famous. It's about nine stories tall! It looks like a castle and reflects against the emerald-green of Lake Superior. The water is so clear you can see the bottom. Wow! When I come back I want to see the Miner's Castle Falls too. And I am coming back to this place!

My second favorite place in the 43 miles of Pictured Rocks was Grand Portal Point. There's a natural bridge under the cliff. I wished I had my own boat so I could explore everything the way I wanted to.

This place looked like the perfect hideaway for pirates. They could just row their boat into the cave.

And the colors of the rock were so beautiful - reddish gold. Maybe there's real gold there. I never thought of that! Think of all the ice cream sundaes I could buy with just a lump or two of that dirt!

My dad said it wasn't gold. I think he just wanted to keep me from diving off the side of the boat. I bet there's all kinds of treasure in that place.